BUGGY RIDDLES

BUGGY RIDDLES

by Katy Hall and Lisa Eisenberg

pictures by Simms Taback

PUFFIN BOOKS

PUFFIN BOOKS
Published by the Penguin Group
Penguin Books USA Inc., 375 Hudson Street, New York, New York 10014, U.S.A.
Penguin Books Ltd, 27 Wrights Lane, London W8 5TZ, England
Penguin Books Australia Ltd, Ringwood, Victoria, Australia
Penguin Books Canada Ltd, 10 Alcorn Avenue, Toronto, Ontario, Canada M4V 3B2
Penguin Books (N.Z.) Ltd, 182–190 Wairau Road, Auckland 10, New Zealand

Penguin Books Ltd, Registered Offices: Harmondsworth, Middlesex, England

First published in the United States of America by Dial Books for Young Readers, 1986
First paperback edition published by Dial Books for Young Readers, 1988
Published in a Puffin Easy-to-Read edition, 1993

1 3 5 7 9 10 8 6 4 2

LIBRARY OF CONGRESS CATALOGING-IN-PUBLICATION DATA
Hall, Katy.
Buggy riddles / by Katy Hall and Lisa Eisenberg;
pictures by Simms Taback.   p.   cm.
Originally published: New York: Dial Books for Young Readers, 1986,
in series: Dial easy-to-read.
Summary: An illustrated collection of insect riddles including
"Why do bees hum? They don't know the words!" and
"What is the best year for grasshoppers? Leap year!"
ISBN 0-14-036543-5
1. Riddles, Juvenile. 2. Insects—Juvenile humor.
[1. Riddles. 2. Insects—Wit and humor.]
I. Eisenberg, Lisa. II. Taback, Simms, ill. III. Title.
PN6371.5.H347   1993
818'.5402–dc20   93-6556   CIP   AC

Reading Level 2.3

To Kate-e-did,
F-Leigh, and
Baby buggy Annie

K.H. and L.E.

To Gail

S.T.

What did the flea say
when the puppy ran away?

Doggone!

Why are frogs so happy?

They eat
whatever bugs them.

What bug is the best
ball player?

The spider.
It's good at catching flies.

What happens when two frogs try to catch the same fly at the same time?

They get tongue-tied!

How do you start
a lightning bug race?

On your mark! Get set! Glow!

How can you keep
a mosquito from biting you
on Monday?

Swat it on Sunday.

Where do flies go to dance?

To the fly ball!

What is the quietest bee?

The mumble bee.

What bug likes picnics,
dresses in a red suit,
and has a white beard?

Ant-a Claus!

What do you call two
spiders who just got
married?

Newly webs!

If dogs have fleas,
what do sheep have?

Fleece!

What does a fruit fly do
in a cornfield?

It goes in one ear and
out the other.

Where do flies get
their news?

From the Daily Fly Paper!

What do you get
if you cross two bees
with a water pistol?

A bee-bee gun.

Why do mosquitoes
make good pets?

They're so tame.
They'll eat right out of your hand!

Where do ants come from?

Antarctica.

How many family members
came to the picnic?

Three sisters, two uncles, and
10,000 ants!

Why do bees hum?

They don't know the words!

How does the queen bee
fix her hair?

With a honeycomb.

What do termites do for a rest?

Take a coffee table break.

What do spiders like
with their hamburgers?

French flies!

Where do bugs go
on vacation?

Timbugtoo!

What do you call a dream in which mosquitoes are attacking you?

A bite-mare.

What do bugs
use Cheerios for?

Hula hoops!

How do bees get to school?

They take the buzz!

What do you say when
you tickle a baby mosquito?

Itchy-kitchy-koo!

What flavor ice cream
do mosquitoes like best?

Vein-illa!

What valentine came to
the hive on February 14?

Honey, bee mine!

Where do moths go
to dance?

The mothball!

Why is it hard for a ladybug to hide?

Because she's always spotted.

What kind of seats
do bugs have in their cars?

Bugget seats.

Why don't flies
fly through screens?

They don't want to
strain themselves.

What did one flea say
to the other?

Shall we walk
or take the greyhound to town?

What did the mosquito say
when she got a stomachache?

It must have been
someone I ate!

What should you tell
a fly that moves into
your sneaker?

Shoe fly, don't bother me!

What do you get when
you cross a caterpillar
and a bee?

A fuzzy yellow jacket!

What is the best year
for grasshoppers?

Leap year!

What do you get
if you cross a centipede
and a parrot?

A walkie-talkie!

Where do sick wasps go?

To the waspital.

What animal has
the most ticks?

A watchdog!

What do bugs have that
no other animal has?

Baby buggies.

On what day do spiders
eat the most?

Flyday!